For Anna and Michael,
first time great-grandparents! D.M.

First published 2021 by Nosy Crow Ltd
The Crow's Nest, 14 Baden Place
Crosby Row, London SE1 1YW
www.nosycrow.com

ISBN 978 1 78800 990 4
Nosy Crow and associated logos are trademarks
and/or registered trademarks of Nosy Crow Ltd.

Text and illustrations copyright © David Melling 2021
The right of David Melling to be identified as the author and illustrator
of this work has been asserted.

A CIP catalogue record for this book is available from the British Library.

Printed in China

Papers used by Nosy Crow are made from wood grown in sustainable forests.

10 9 8 7 6 5 4 3 2 1

Ruffles

and the **teeny, tiny kittens**

David Melling

This is **Ruffles.**

Ruffles **loves** . . .

singing . . .   scratching . . .   eating . . .

fetching . . .   sniffing . . .   chewing . . .

digging . . .   running . . .   and sleeping.

But Ruffles **does not love**
the teeny, tiny kittens.

They climb . . .

and hide . . .

and pounce . . .

and purr . . .

and lick . . .

and snore . . .

and stare . . .

and chase . . .

and poo.

The teeny, tiny kittens follow Ruffles **everywhere**.

They want to do **everything** that Ruffles does.

But Ruffles doesn't like sharing . . .

not his snacks . . .

not his cushion . . .

not his tree . . .

not his window . . .

not his hole . . .

not his stick . . .

not his chew . . .

not his basket . . .

or his favourite ball.

And Ruffles **really** doesn't want to share

Big Blue Blankie.

Big Blue Blankie is where Ruffles
likes to snuggle up and feel cosy.

But the teeny, tiny kittens love Big Blue Blankie, too.

They climb . . .

and hide . . .

and pounce . . .

and purr . . .

and lick . . .

and snore . . .

and stare . . .

and chase . . .

and poo.

Ruffles wants Big Blue Blankie back,
but the teeny, tiny kittens don't understand.

They think it's a game!

Until . . .

R

ip!!!

Oh no! Big Blue Blankie is torn in two!

Ruffles takes Not-So-Big Blue Blankie to his basket.
He wants to snuggle up and feel cosy.

But Not-So-Big Blue Blankie is **too small.**

Ruffles shivers . . .   and wriggles . . .   and twists . . .

and turns . . .   until the . . .   teeny, tiny kittens . . .

snuggle up . . .   to keep . . .   him cosy.

In the morning, the teeny, tiny kittens are playing.
Ruffles wants to play, too . . .

so he fetches his favourite ball.

Playing . . .   is . . .   so . . .

much . . .   more . . .   fun . . .

when . . .   you . . .   share.

Ruffles and the teeny, tiny kittens are **friends!**

Ruffles loves . . .

singing . . .

scratching . . .

eating . . .

fetching . . .

sniffing . . .

chewing . . .

digging . . .

running . . .

and sharing.

But most of all, Ruffles **loves**
the teeny, tiny kittens. Well . . .

most of the time.